I0601563

Pest of a Bug Work Humor

just Deirdre.

COPYRIGHT

Copyright © 2019 by just Deirdre. All rights reserved. No part of this book may be used or reproduced without written permission, except for brief quotations in critical articles and reviews.

This is a work of fiction. Names, characters, places, and incidents are either the product of the author's imagination or are used fictitiously, and any resemblance to any actual persons, living or dead, events or locales is entirely coincidental.

First Edition, Published 2019 Printed in the United States of America

ISBN-13: 978-1-7339521-6-3 ebook
ISBN-13: 978-1-7339521-0-1 Paperback
Library of Congress Control Number: 2019904114

Pest of a Bug: Work Humor Written by just Deirdre.
Published by Deirdre Braud
www.petitebreaux.com
Cover Design by Sam (Illustrationalpal) Johnson
Edited by Michelle Rascon
EditorRascon.com

Dedication

For Frankie Mae, Glynedra, Glynnis, Delloid (Ajamu) Sr., Sharon, NaRiyah, Delloid dj Jr, Deven (Tunde), Shuni (Ella Mae), Demetrius, Earl and my granddog HoneyBun(HB). You give me purpose.

Pest of a Bug

A sudden flood incident had destroyed Inner City Ant Colony, leaving them without a home. The day the flood happened; none would have guessed such calamity would befall their colony. The ants had woken up that morning going about their daily activities in high spirits. The sun had shone on them, and the skies were clear with no sign of what was to come.

The rains had started. It was so unexpected that most continued their activities thinking the light showers would let up. The showers increased just as suddenly as the rains began to surge heavier pelts. Soon, before their very eyes, the rain washed away everything the members of the colony held dear.

All the ant families that existed in Inner City were still below ground, surrounded by only mudslides, barely alive. Some were rummaging through the mud trying to gather whatever they could salvage from the muddy ruin. The day that started looking so bright ended with them losing everything they called their own. Disaster had struck.

It was no use; everything had gone up the river with the floodwater. Several ants lost; several injured with no hospital available for treatment. Survivors were traveling in a single column trying to find signs of daylight so they could crawl above ground to start anew.

The journey wouldn't be easy. It meant a long trek to the closest colony; three days of travel they weren't equipped for. Physically and emotionally, they were not suited for this new lease on life they looked for – so unexpected, so unprepared. Much of the colony had never traveled outside of Inner City. It would take a strong will, the bravest of mindsets and a lot of hope for them to conquer these tough times.

Despite the misfortune and the challenging situation, the ants marched on with persistence. Theirs was a strength born within. Despite the hard times, the colony would push through.

Abruptly, a worker with a stout body shouted, "Hey, everyone! Look up ahead! Light!"

This instantaneously raised the morale of the tired soldier ants relentlessly heading the traveling colony. They quickly marched ahead to check it out.

"Okay, now. Wait a minute!" said Steven, a gangly looking male ant wearing eyeglasses over his large protruding eyes, as he jumped in front to stop them. With baseball cap perched on his head and one antenna pointed up, he stood on his hind legs and pleaded, "Just hear me out please…" as they all kept marching on around him. One ant with an injured leg, walking briskly with the support of a tree twig, replied,

"Move, Steven. No one wants to hear what you have to say."

Another, with a fractured thorax, quipped, "Not today, man. Get out of the way."

"I'm only trying to help," Steven protested. If only they would stop and listen to him. They hardly ever heeded what he had to say. He complained to the Commander and other bugs in higher positions about everything. Often, he had their interest at heart.

"Yeah, right! We do not need your kind of help today, Steven. All you do is complain," countered another with a red scarf tied to her right hind leg.

"He's a butthole," retorted the ant with one crutch, now up ahead as they all continued toward the light. The primary goal was getting to the promised land, not listening to the rumblings of a renowned complainer.

The General marched ahead and stood right beneath the spot where the light shone down. He gazed into the brightness to confirm if the opening was safe enough to navigate through. The General thought the light at the end of the tunnel was a train making its way through. He did not want to be the one who would lead his colony to their death.

Drops of water splashed on his temple. Startled, he shook his head from side to side. The light was not an oncoming train, but a way out. In a twisting motion, he turned around to the soldiers who stared at him with interest. "It's all clear. Bring the rest of the colony up. We will form a ladder and climb out," the General shouted with anticipation.

Everyone trooped forward the minute they heard the instructions. Each ant linked with another to form the required ladder. There was a way around these things; the ants had a method of "looking after" their citizens in times like this. The injured, the elderly, women and children were the first that went up the self- made ladder. Antennas and intertwined hind legs connected until everyone was above ground.

"Stay close together everyone!" the General ordered.

As they examined the environment that surrounded them, distress crossed their faces. Not knowing which way to start their journey, they felt lost and helpless. Muddy debris everywhere, nothing looked familiar. This was nothing like the promised land they were expecting to find. Another wasteland, much like the one left behind. Something better up ahead was the hope. They had to keep going to reach it.

"Does anyone know what direction we should go?" a dispirited voice from behind asked.

Some stood still, as others turned around in circles searching for answers. Even the General was quiet.

"Excuse me!" Steven cried, pushing through the crowd, nudging ants in the side as he came forward.

"Excuse me, excuse me," he repeated, his tall, lanky frame towering above everyone. They did not seem ready or willing to listen to him, but he would not give them a choice. Steven would make them listen to him whether they wanted to or not. "I know you all think I don't know what I am talking about, but, see this." He pulled something flat, round, and shiny from his pocket. "Err, what's that?" asked the old male ant with the walking stick. Murmurs of curiosity rippled through the gathered crowd.

"One winter while scouting for food in the woods, I found this gadget. Out where those humans hunt animals," Steven replied low-key.

"Err, okay, but what is it, Steven?" again asked the old ant.

"Well," he opened the lid, "they called it a compass, it tells you which way is north, south, east, and west." That would teach them to listen to him whenever he spoke. He reckoned this would earn him another level of respect from the other ants. Baffled murmurs of "Huh?!" "Ooohh!" and "What?!" rippled through the gathered crowd as each tried to get a close look at the weird object. All at once, they wanted to be close to him and the object he held. As guessed, he reached celebrity status.

"So, now, which way we headin', brother soldier?" asked the female ant with the red scarf.

The General, speechless for a moment, studied the compass in Steven's possession.

Steven tilted the compass this way and that, saying, "Let's get these ants on the road, Papi!" He laughed at his own awkward joke as he lowered the compass for all to see. They watched as the arrow in the compass trembled, shook, and turned. Finally, it stopped, then pointed to the west.

"This is the direction we should begin our journey," he told the General.

The General doubted Steven because of his history, but this was actionable intel he could act on. Due to the dire nature of their situation, he didn't want to be the blame. So, he went along with it. How bad could it get?

"We are heading west. Let's move out!" the General declared, facing the crowd, and pointing westward.

"You heard the man, let's move!" Steven said, mimicking the General's tone of voice. He planned to milk this new status as much as he could. The colony could withdraw from him within the twinkling of an eye.

"See? I told y'all I could help, but you didn't wanna listen to me," he bragged, showing those big bug eyes and grinning. He might as well turn the knife in the wound by reminding them he brought the solution to the problem.

*****

They traveled four days and three nights before reaching Outer City Ant Colony. Steven had talked over everybody that was around him. He ate their heads off with unnecessary talks he felt were necessary to tide them over. To him, talking about anything and everything did them a favor, taking their minds off the walk ahead. He didn't grasp that he made them tired. With no idea where they were headed, the walk alone was exhausting. Adding Steven and his yapping was an ordeal worse than they could bear.

"You know, the day I found that strange instrument, which is saving us, I thought to myself, 'Steven, sonny, today will be amazing. The sun is bright. The day is clear. Something good is about to happen.' Never would have thought my find would be such a great masterpiece," he said, speaking at the top of his voice. Only the elderly ant who needed a stick to support himself listened beside Steven.

"You see," he started to say again to the utmost chagrin of the old ant.

"Why you botherin' me, Steven! Find the Queen to bother. Go away."

"I ain't bothering you, sir. I'm telling you the amazing story of our survival." He meant every word of what he said. How could the elderly ant accuse him of pestering, when all Steven was doing was keeping him company? He did not even consider Steven's celebrity status.

"Go bother someone your own age," the ant said, swatting him away with his stick.

And so, Steven went in search of another prey. He continued to move around from worker to soldier ants, boring them with one story or another. They chased him away, insulted him, threw things at him, but Steven stuck with them regardless.

The colony felt disappointed when they arrived at their destination. This was not the Outer City they were coming to, to take refuge. This place was worse than a wasteland. There were diverse types of debris floating around. The rain had swept away most buildings and the few still standing were half destroyed. Every ant from Inner City fell over themselves in despair. Even Steven could not speak, his glory was taken away by the harsh realities of what they were facing. Of what use was the instrument he had found if it had led them to a wasteland?

The General was at a loss on what was happening and what to do. They had left their own ruins in their own part of town, seeking hope and a better settlement.

But here they were experiencing the very same thing. He decided it was best if he went in search of the members of the colony.

"What will we do now? The whole place is a horrible mess. They don't even have their own place together. How can we stay here with them if they don't have a home themselves?" one ant complained. This saddened the General.

"Hold on, fellow ants. Let us not lose hope yet. I will go out there in search of any sign of life. We can still get help. I want three able-bodied ants to follow me in search of the ants of Outer City Ant Colony."

As he spoke, not one ant volunteered. It was as though they had lost every iota of energy left in them.

After two minutes, no ant stepped forward. Finally, a hand raised, and he heaved a sigh of relief until he noticed it was Steven. The General wanted to run as far away from this ant as possible.

"Well, Steven, you should stay back and help with the weak and injured," the General said to him as he approached.

"Aw, hell naw. Let Steven go with you! We are fine the way we are. We have other able-bodied ants who can take care of us. It's best if he goes with you," someone shouted from the back.

The General had no choice but to take Steven with him on the search. The General made him promise not to utter a word. They didn't have to walk too far before they came across some worker ants already rebuilding their city. It was amazing to watch them work in unison. The ants worked based on the chain of command. Some built homes, others collected materials and tended to others that were sick. The injured were few. It also looked as though they were fast with their rebuilding. The General and Steven walked up to the red ant and introduced themselves. They then asked to see Queen Mara.

When the ant heard where they were from, he snapped to attention and took them to the Queen. One glance at the General and Steven, a worker ant scurried around in search of food for the visitors. The General told the Queen details of their destroyed colony and ants injured or dead. He added that they needed help with housing.

"Why, I am sorry to hear that, General. We also suffered damage. Yet, we didn't endure quite as much as you. The worker ants have been working nonstop to rebuild our colony."

"I can see that."

"We have to rebuild your colony as well. There isn't much here to give to you. We have some food stored, and I had hoped that would be enough until we finish rebuilding both. Take as much food as needed back to your colony."

"That would be great. My colony would be grateful."

"We need to have a meeting with each Bug Commander to work out the details of how to rebuild your colony."

And with that, the Inner-City ants carried a food supply and a working team to help rebuild their city. The ants were glad they did not have to move to Outer City. At once, the news was sent out to all corners of the towns about the need to hold an emergency meeting. It would take place in Outer City as there was nowhere to have the meeting in Inner City. As soon as the news got out, the colonies invited for the meeting turned up in numbers. It was the bug way, you see; helping one another in time of need and putting the needs of the weak first. Commanders from each Bug section met at Outer City Ant Colony to hold an emergency meeting. They discussed how best to work together to rebuild Inner City Ant Colony. In attendance was the Queen of Outer City, Head Sergeant at Arms of Inner City, the General, Queen Bee from up north, and Black Widow Spider from above ground. The General kept reminding everyone that his colony had been washed away and had nowhere to go. Each chose their best workers to work in Outer City's Disaster Response office.

Queen Bee chose one of her brightest members, Desiree, as Project Manager. "Desiree, a small bee but works hard. She's dedicated and can get the job done."

The General from Inner City chose Steven to process all necessary documentation. "He is great with speaking on behalf of all bugs, and very political. Steven slacks and may not be as hard of a worker as your Desiree, but he has an eye for details and knows how to work a crowd."

The General did not add that Steven could be annoying to work with. He was great at the things the General had listed, but that didn't stop him from being a pest anyway. The General hoped that the people he worked with could see the good in Steven and not bash his head.

Black Widow Spider called in one of her newbies, Gretchen, from up top. "She is much older and needs to keep active. But she is a bookworm, this one. Her nose is always buried in one leaf book or another despite her age. Let her file and make delivery rounds so she can get the hang of how Disaster Response works."

Created for rebuilding, selected workers would live below ground in Outer Colony, in a small office station with living quarters. They made a backup plan to have their next best workers on standby if Desiree or Steven needed replacing. Memos were sent to all heads of the Bug colonies to help in rebuilding Inner City Ant Colony. Much was destroyed by the flood; food, shelter, and entire families were all gone. It was not only the ants that came to help; all varied species of insects did, too – spiders, bees, the list was endless.

As the workers functioned together to rebuild, moving dirt, and breaking twigs to make new nests, the heads watched over. Two small office cubicles were built for Desiree and Steven, and a small area for Gretchen with a desk and supplies. There was also a break room area for the workers. Gretchen made deliveries from up top and carried all memos to above ground heads from Steven. She also kept supplies inventory and the break room area well stocked with food and water.

In a week, Inner City Ant Colony was abuzz already with Outer City Disaster Response office workers. The displaced members of Inner City lived above ground of Outer City Ant Colony in stitched leaf shelters built by bees and spiders. Food was brought to them by the worker ants from Outer City and other colonies. Some of the Inner City worker ants regained their strength and joined in the search for food and other supplies. It was a coordinated process.

*****

Desiree buzzed herself down the tunnel dug for entry to the building where she was working at Inner City Ant Colony. She opened the wooden door, flew in, tucked in her little wings, and landed softly on the mud floor of her cubicle. Bees didn't do so well below ground like the ants did so this task would be a challenge, and Desiree was careful. She looked around at the area where she would be working. There stood a half-finished cubicle with a desk, a chair, and a computer. She had a family above ground that lived miles away, but she didn't want to think about them right now; she was here to help. All bugs pulled together, they had something in common – they all lived off the land, whether it was above ground or below ground.

Her official workday began in the morning. She did not know the other two bugs that worked in the makeshift cubicles beside her but hoped they were the friendly sort. She took the duffel bag from her wings, set it down on the desk, and removed its contents: a photo frame of her husband, two kids, and the few trophies she earned from work among the ant and bee communities.

She sat down in her chair, adjusting herself to fit without snarling her hind wings as she tucked them inward. *This shouldn't be too bad for a month. It seems as if it will be quiet and I will get to make new friends.* Desiree rearranged her table with the items she had taken out of her duffel bag and checked her calendar for tasks to complete in the coming days. She gathered her duffel bag and swung it over her wings. *Tomorrow will begin a new day.* Then she flew out the tiny office through the tunnel, heading home to prepare herself for her new work life as Project Manager. A little surprised that neither of the other co-bugs that would be working on the project had shown up, but it didn't bother her much. She had always been more hardworking than many of the other bugs in her colony, so why would any other insect be any different? They were not as conscientious as she was. That did not make them lousy insects. They would show up tomorrow when the actual work would start.

Desiree awoke extra early the following day. Thrilled about her new task at hand, she buzzed around her apartment as she prepared to head out to work. Her husband would help with taking care of their baby honeybees until her return. It was about an hour's flight. She figured it would be smooth as she had no heavy luggage to weigh her down. She had dropped by her office and dropped off overnight luggage the previous day.

Grabbing her latte-filled bottle off the kitchen counter, she drifted to the door and took flight after she had locked the door behind her. The weather was warm, the wind blew, there was some dew in the air, and daylight was approaching. The day would be fantastic.

She could not wait to meet with her colleagues and to make a difference. She enjoyed the cool breeze blowing in her face as she avoided trees, flying leaves, and other floating debris.

As she approached Inner City, she saw the opening to the underground tunnel. Desiree braced her wings behind her in a tucking motion, checked out the area, went straight in, antennas pointed and staring downward. Picking up speed, she flew like a rocket through the tunnel. On approach to her office, slow and steady, she came to a perfect landing. She stood straight, shaking her wings out. Out of nowhere, she got struck from behind – hard! It landed her face flat in the mud followed by a loud, dull *thud-thud*.

She flipped onto her back, moaning in pain, and looked around to see what had knocked her off her feet. Hovering over her, chewing gum loudly, she saw this tall, skinny, big-eyed male ant with eyeglasses and a baseball cap on. Desiree was beyond mad. She felt a rage spread through her body to her wings like none she had ever felt before.

"Are you all right?" Steven asked as he extended one front ant leg down to help her up.

Ignoring his outstretched leg, she leaned back onto her forelegs and pushed herself off the ground, firing at Steven a barrage of questions: "What in the hell is wrong with you?

Why did you race through the tunnel at such stupid speed behind me without stopping? Were you trying to knock me over? Look at me all dirty, are you happy now? Who are you by the way?"

In her mind, she thought, *thankfully no one is here yet. Maybe I can quickly go back home or go to the workers' living quarters to clean up and change. But damn it, I did not plan for this. Too damn early for this!* There were a lot of reasons for her to be mad aside from the fact that her head was throbbing. She didn't like days with a bad start like this. It made things feel as though it would be bad throughout the day. That and the fact that she liked to think herself a neat little bug. She hated anything that caused her to be dirty, and that was what this individual had done to her.

Steven straightened, transferring most of his weight to his hind legs. He replied to Desiree's questions with a question, "Who are you?" and continued, "I'm supposed to be here. I work here."

Desiree was even more annoyed than initially. He had not only done what he did, but he was also rude. Too rude for her liking.

"Well, I do too!" she fired back. "I am the Project Manager in charge here," she retorted, pointing to the badge pinned to her thorax with her name and title on it. "Okay, Ms. Desiree. I am Steven, in charge of all communications, grievances, and complaints. So, I guess it's you and me. No… and one other.

We have somewhat of a clerk. Her name is Gretchen. Guess she hasn't arrived yet. I hear she is a much older woman."

She had to smile despite herself. For an offender, he sure knows how not to apologize.

"Hmm. Nice to know, Steven, and it is interesting to meet you albeit awkwardly. Later, Steven," she said to him as she walked to her cubicle to wipe off the dirt. When she was done, she went straight to resume her duties. There was so much to do.

Two hours after midday, Steven was back at Desiree's cubicle standing tall and lanky. He leaned over to Desiree, speaking in a near-whisper, "Look, I asked the Master Ant Sergeant to hire Sal, my cousin, and he said they had no more openings and Sal wasn't qualified. I go outside this morning to check on the progress of the construction and guess what I found out? The Sergeant has his worker ant son, his uncle Bee- in-law, and nephew all working out there. Next, they'll have the whole Honey Comb working. I questioned when they were hired and – here's the kicker, Desiree – they started when this construction began!"

Desiree smiled to him, at a loss as to how she should react to this ant. "No, not the whole Honey Comb. There is no such thing. You're exaggerating. You know how it is, Steven. Why are you so surprised about these things? Do some work and get away from my desk. I am not indulging you today. It's the first day at work, and we should work hard," she replied. "Not just today though," she added when she realized Steven might interpret her statement as something else. "Every day until we are done building your colony."

"I'm sure going to be writing my report this week already. This is some nepotism gone wild for sure," he replied, smirking. "So, who do you have in the Bug government, Desiree?"

Desiree rolled her eyes, shaking her head as she replied, "Steven, I don't have anyone. Every time I tried; it was the same answer: 'Have them apply.'"

"See? See? They not fair," Steven lamented. "But now I'm in on this one. The nepotism for this rebuilding project must stop."

"Okay, Steven," she said, already tired of where this conversation was going. She did not want to be drawn into his drama. She changed the topic to something work related instead. "Can you write some letters to the divisional head on the progress and things needed to keep the construction going? I will continue with the financial part, making sure we collect all the money needed to complete this construction. Or don't you want your colony rebuilt?"

"Yeah, yeah, sure I do. I will work on the letters. But you know, the whole setup here, it's not fair. We were all handpicked," Steven said with a hint of frustration.

"I know. Look, I want this project finished so that I can go back to my home. I am not here for much else."

Steven liked to talk and wasn't as eager as she was to help get his colony rebuilt. Desiree was not for unnecessary chatter, so she wasn't comfortable with the idea of talking nonstop with this ant.

"Well, just so you know, I'm 'bout to take off. I've got some Bug Workers' Union duties today," he replied.

"Bug Union?!" Desiree asked surprised. She queried, "You in that too?"

"Yep," he replied, smiling.

"Jeez, Steven! When do you plan on working? Even when you're here, you are not exactly working. You are on the phone half the time." *What is wrong with this ant?* she thought to herself.

"Look here," he said as he leaned in, antennas curled over, staring down at her with big bug eyes. "I'm not telling you how to work. So, don't worry 'bout what I'm doing. You're just jealous." He turned on his lanky legs and walked away out of the office.

Desiree shook her bee head and went back to work. This would be one annoying team member to work with. She could already feel the tension headaches from talking to him for this long. She hoped he changed this behavior. She didn't know if she would last working aside him.

*****

The project ran smoothly onsite. But the same couldn't be said for behind the scenes. Steven was a big problem for Desiree. He never seemed interested in doing any work. Instead of working, he was always talking loudly on the phone with friends and family.

And, as usual, he was on the phone again, this time with a lady named Delores, one of the government executives from one of the many colonies above ground in Inner City.

He said, "So, Delores, check this out..." and launched into one of his many stories, laughing intermittently with the lady. After the call, he got up from his seat and went over to Desiree's desk, bent over her shoulder, and said, "Desiree, guess what?"

Desiree kept working, ignoring him. She was not in the mood for all this nonsense – especially not today. She didn't like the laxness Steven employed with work, and she would not let him drag her into his foolishness. Soon, though, she changed her mind and looked up at him.

"What?" she said.

"I'm going on vacation for two days next week," he declared.

Surprised, she asked, "How is that possible? Didn't we just start working less than a month ago?"

He smiled coyly, saying, "Yeah, I know. I got it like that." He then snapped his fingers, asking with a laugh, "Don't you wish you did too?" He laughed a little too loudly. "Babe, I know bugs; highly placed bugs."

"Please go away, Steven. You are distracting me, and I am busy. Just get away from my desk. You are such a pest," replied Desiree.

"No, that's where you're incorrect, honeybee, I'm a bug!" Steven teased as he playfully sauntered away laughing; a laugh that Desiree found annoying.

Desiree needed something to distract her from the anger boiling inside her. She knew just the thing. As a fitness buff, Desiree worked out as much as possible despite her schedule. She kept a ten-pound kettlebell at her desk to lift during the day as a form of muscle exercise for her slender forelegs. She got up from her desk to spread her wings, something she rarely ever did while below ground. She felt stressed and tried to stretch out her tensed body to feel relaxed. This Steven character was testing every centimeter of her sanity.

*****

Desiree sat at her desk trying to get work done before the day ended. Her to-do list had about ten items when the day started. It was just past lunch, and she had ticked eight things off the to-do list. Besides this, she wanted to do work before Steven came back from his many errands.

Steven had made a daily habit of coming to her cubicle cracking dry jokes only he laughed at, saying silly things she didn't consider proper in a work environment. She even avoided going to the break room whenever he was there, preferring to eat at her desk in her cubicle. Sadly, for her, the office arrangement of her cubicle directly opposite Steven's only made matters worse for her. To Steven, it was all fun and chitchat with a fellow co-worker.

When Steven came back from his errands, Desiree usually kept to her side of the office space and sometimes even missed lunch because he was around. It seemed to work fine until one day, just before his self- imposed vacation when he had bothered her again.

"Look, Steven, I am not in the mood at all today," she retorted as Steven began his playful banter.

The thing with Steven was simple. Steven didn't think he was annoying or irritating, he thought he was funny! He knew deep down that his jokes were funny. He laughed at them so why shouldn't other people?

"Aw, such a spoilsport, you boring bug. I'm trying to lighten up the moment here. Make you laugh," he replied, perched on the edge of her desk.

"Thank you, Steven, but I don't need you to lighten up the moment. My moment was simply fine until you arrived. We are here to work not catch fun, okay? Now please go to your desk because unlike you, some of us here that do not know bugs in high places actually have work to do."

"Such bitterness!" Steven said, bursting into laughter and further irritating Desiree. But he wasn't done. He continued to pester her.

"What happened to your sense of humor, honeybee? Marriage must have killed it, no doubt."

Desiree was hot with anger. His comments were starting to really get to her. She knew she had to do something before he made her angrier than she already was. "One more silly comment about me, Steven, and I will gut punch you!" Desiree threatened with crossed antennas.

But for some weird reason, Steven didn't see the need to stop, did not think he crossed the line. He kept talking. "Wow, threatening violence in the office? Is it that bad at home now, Desiree?" he teased as he slid off her desk, walking back to his desk. "File a complaint, dear Ms. Desiree. That is why I am here. Except you can't complain to me about me, now can you?" he said as he settled his lanky frame onto his seat, laughing at his own crude joke.

Desiree had considered reporting him to someone if he continued with this annoying behavior of his. But now that he spoke of it, she realized it was a lost cause. There was absolutely no one to report to since he took all the complaints.

"Can't do nothing, Desiree?" he cooed. "Snitches get stitches."

That was it, she could not take it anymore. She made good on her threat. She gripped her kettlebell, jumped on her six legs with wings outstretched, flew right at Steven, and swung the kettlebell straight at his head. The kettlebell connected with Steven's upper jaw making a loud crunching sound as his head hit his desk, knocking him out cold.

He fell out of his chair and crumpled to a heap on the ground. Gretchen, who had been quiet all along and never interfered when he pestered Desiree, peeked from around the corner of her cubicle and turned away quickly. She exclaimed, "I knew it! I just knew this was coming. I knew it was coming. He is such a pain in the butt!"

Gretchen felt it in her bones that Desiree would hit this Steven guy one day. She had watched how Steven made it a point of duty to pester the bee since they had started working. Steven had spared her. And because she was a bug who liked to mind her business, she didn't see the need to interfere in their matter. She sometimes thought that Desiree had encouraged him at some point. But the way Desiree rebuffed the man made her change her mind about it. And now, it had happened. Steven had gotten his head bashed in.

Desiree buzzed back to her desk, tucked her wings, and sat down to continue working as if nothing had happened. She knew Steven had only fainted – which was her aim really, to knock him out and shut him up, the tough bastard, a small kettlebell could cause no serious harm to his thick skull. She put on her headphones and hummed to the tune of the music playing on her computer.

Gretchen called in the head of security, Marcus, to explain that an accident just happened. He was confused at first and asked her what to do because Steven could be dead. But upon closer examination, he found him to be breathing. Steven had only fainted from a sharp, painful blow to the head.

Marcus said he would contact the Inner City Ant Colony doctor, saying, "They know how to patch up their own."

Gretchen strolled around to Steven's desk to get a better look. She said, "My, my, what a knockout." She got a towel from the break room and wrapped Steven's head with it to stop the bleeding from a small cut on the side of his head. The office doors swung open as the ant doctor, and two other ants with a stretcher came in. After some time checking out the ant and his head injury…

"He is fine, just unconscious from a trauma to the head. Nothing we can do for him here, we need to get him home to the colony hospital to stitch the wound," the doctor said after observing Steven, who was still out cold. The other two gently picked Steven up, laid him on the stretcher, and wheeled him out. They put the cot on a lever so he could be hoisted up above ground.

Throughout the whole exchange between Marcus, Gretchen, and the doctor, Desiree never once glanced up to see what was going on. She felt calm, enjoyed her music and the quietness as she worked. It was as though a *weight* had been lifted off her chest. Gretchen cleared the scattered contents and documents in Steven's cubicle, piling them neatly in an office box and sealing it.

After tidying up Steven's cubicle, Gretchen ambled her eight spider legs around to Desiree's desk. Desiree, unaware that Gretchen was standing there, kept working and listening to the music through her headphones. Gretchen taped her lightly on the antenna, which startled her because she thought it was Steven again. Tensing, she turned her neck quickly to react but calmed down when she saw it was only Gretchen.

"Sorry to startle you," Gretchen said. "I am so glad you shut him up. I never said anything, but he was so annoying. Such a disturbance."

"I really didn't mean to hurt him, Gretchen. It just came from quick reflexes that had built up from the anger of enduring all his sarcasm and crude inappropriate jokes. Hopefully, when he is back, he will be serious now, and we can get some work done in peace and quiet," Desiree replied, speaking for the first time since the incident happened.

"I hope so too," responded Gretchen as she buzzed slowly back to her cubicle, thinking, *That girl done bashed that Steven's head in good. If Chief Commander Ant gets notice of this, construction may come to a halt.*

*****

That evening after her work shift, Gretchen was in her quarters eating a meal of raw honey with crackers, watching Bug TV, when a knock sounded on her door.

"Yeah, come in, Desiree," she said. She knew it was Desiree as they were the only two in these quarters; all other workers had separate quarters at the other end of the tunnel layer.

"Gretchen, can I come sit and watch TV with you? It's lonely down here," Desiree said.

"Sure, sure, Desiree. I understand how that feels. Do have a seat, dear," replied Gretchen who was now finishing her meal.

Desiree tucked her wings and settled in the recliner by the side of Gretchen's bed. Gretchen pulled out her needlework from under her pillow. She had been webbing a baby spider web blanket for one of her daughters carrying a large egg sac. Gretchen had eight daughters and a son. Desiree looked on, impressed as she spun the web. After some female chitchat, they both retired for the night with Desiree heading back to her own sleeping quarters.

*****

Early the next morning, both women were up and ready for work. With Steven off duty, there was much more to do now. Gretchen was in first and had made coffee.

"Morning, Gretchen!" Desiree buzzed, settling smoothly onto her chair.

"Hey, morning, Desiree," Gretchen replied, smiling.

"Have the workers been in to punch their time cards yet?" asked Desiree.

Gretchen stuck her head out the doorway to look around the corridor to see if anyone was in the tunnels working. She listened intently for a while but heard nothing, then turned back in. She shook her head at Desiree saying, "None yet."

Desiree grabbed a cup of coffee, tasted it with her tongue, then took a sip, and sighed with pleasure. "Thanks, Gretchen. I needed this coffee this morning," she said as she stepped out into the working area. *Where is everyone?* she wondered as she stretched out her wings and buzzed over to the workers' quarters down the long tunnel layer. There, she found them all still asleep.

She was surprised. What was wrong with everyone? Why didn't anyone take their jobs seriously around here? Trying to wake them up, she shouted, "Hey, guys, why aren't we up in the tunnels working already?"

One worker ant rolled over and continued sleeping. Another half-opened her eyes, raised her head, rubbed her eyes to focus on the source of the noise interrupting her sleep, and asked sleepily, "Why are you here, Ms. De… Desiree?"

"Call me Desiree, please," she replied, taking another soothing sip of her coffee, and continued, "I am here because you all are late starting your shifts this morning."

"Well, Mrs. Desiree, oh, err, sorry, Desiree. I guess you are not aware, it is our off-day today."

"Off-day?!" Desiree exclaimed. "We don't have off-days on this project. We need to get this colony up and running. Your colony for that matter. I have a home that needs and misses me. You should be up and running trying to build your own home once again."

"Look, you better check with Chief Commander Ant, Des, De, Desiree. Whatever. I'm going back to sleep, so keep it quiet, please. Thank you." With that, she pulled up her leaf blanket and went back to sleep.

Desiree flew back through the tunnel to her cubicle at incredible speed, somehow managing not to spill her coffee on the way. She buzzed into her cubicle with visible rage, landing at her desk with a *thump*. Dropping the still-warm cup, she rummaged through some documents arranged on her desk, scattering them as she tried to find the project schedule sheet, she had been using all week.

Gretchen popped in her head. "What is it? Everything okay?" she asked, having grown accustomed to Desiree's careful, quiet landing.

Desiree replied, "I was just told by one of the workers that today is their off-day."

"Oh! Totally forgot about that," Gretchen gasped. "Yeah, the tunnel workers now get one day off per week so they can rest and replenish themselves. All other workers are on today, though," she explained.

Desiree was fuming. "Gretchen..." she moaned, sounding pained. "Why didn't you say anything last night? I mean, I could have rested longer myself this morning, you know."

"I absolutely forgot to mention it, dear. So sorry," Gretchen replied somberly. "It was posted on the noticeboard all through yesterday, so I didn't think to mention it. I guess you must have missed it or something."

Desiree dropped the papers on the desk and picked up the cup of coffee in her little bee hands, taking a single swig to empty the container. "It's okay. I'm here already, no point complaining. I might as well get some work done in the meantime," she said, smiling contritely at Gretchen.

Gretchen smiled back, ambling over to her cubicle. Out of her eight legs, only two were good. She suffered from arthritis badly and had been told often that she needed to have those dead legs amputated, but she vehemently refused, preferring to drag them around like dead weight, which was why she often walked so slowly.

As she walked to her cubicle, grumbling," Don't know why she's mad 'cause tunnel workers get a day off. Shouldn't we all get a day off? It's like she wants to work everyone to death here. Too much dedication. Where did she come from anyway? These bees like work too much, but she's not gonna bother me. I ain't gonna let her. My job here is to file and get the mail out and help with a few other things, that's all."

By the next morning, everyone was at work, and the construction project was running along smoothly. The construction workers in the tunnel were building structures and laying foundations while workers above ground brought in finished nest housings for installation.

Desiree was at her desk looking over contracts and floor plans, making sure all was on schedule. She had her earbuds in, wings tucked back behind her, in her own world. Gretchen was at the copier machine making copies and sending letters out to the Head Commanders with updates.

The door suddenly swung open as tall, lanky Steven sauntered in like he owned the place. "Hey, people! I'm baaack!" he chirped, a big smile on his face. He waved at Gretchen as he passed, saying, "What's up, Gretchen? Miss me? Still dragging those legs, I see. W'sup with that?"

Gretchen looked up, startled as the door closed behind him. She noticed a small bandage on the left side of his head, but otherwise, he seemed fine. Great even, looking refreshed and well rested.

"Steven!" she greeted and swallowed, hesitated, then said, "Hey, you're back, wasn't sure how soon you would be back."

She rapped on the side of the cubicle, trying to get Desiree's attention but no luck, her headphones were plugged in. She was not sure if she should be happy about Steven's return or if she was supposed to be sad.

One thing was sure; things would never be the same as they were when he was not around.

Steven walked to his cubicle, turned to Gretchen in surprise and asked, "Hey! What is this? Why is my cubicle all cleared up and empty? Where is my stuff?" Gazing at her accusingly, he asked, "You did this, didn't ya, Gretchen? Thought I wasn't coming back, yeah?"

She smiled at him with a look of disdain, and replied, "Yes, I didn't want any of your stuff to go missing. It is all in an office box under your desk with documents and files. Nothing was tampered with or displaced, I assure you."

Inside of her, she was not filled with the sweetness she was showing him. She was seething. He was such a horrid little pest who appreciated nothing anyone did. She wondered how the people in his colony ever dealt with him for so long without wanting to wring his neck. Nodding, he smiled back and said, "Err... okay, good one." He playfully blew her a kiss as he tossed his sling bag on the desk and walked around the side to Desiree's cubicle.

Gretchen shook her and turned back to her work. *What a piece of work this guy was! If only he knew...* she thought as the copier hummed back to life.

Steven lightly tapped Desiree on the shoulder as he got to her cubicle, standing behind her with a big smile on his face. "Hey you. Guess who's back? Didn't think I'd be back so soon, right?" he asked mischievously.

Desiree remained cool and didn't turn around just yet to look at Steven. Staring at her screen, surprised at his return, an expression of *What the hell?!* on her face. She blinked her eyes. Seconds later, Steven still standing there, she turned in her chair to face him and said in a calm tone, "Hey, you're back, Steven. Glad to see that you're fine."

"Really? You sure you're glad I'm okay and back? I doubt that, Desiree," he smirked. Then, he continued talking before Desiree could respond. "Yeah, you thought you had gotten rid of me, but you did me a favor. I got to go up top for a while to rest and relax away from all the noise here. After they patched me up, no thanks to you," he pointed to the small bandage on his head, "I got some quality TV time, ate some tasty food, and enjoyed some sunlight. A needed vacation, albeit a painful one." He frowned at her.

Desiree kept a straight face, although she was shaking her head and rolling her eyes in her mind, thinking, *boy, here we go again!* Aloud, she said, "Well, Steven, welcome back. And I'm glad you're okay. Yes, I didn't expect to see you back this soon, but lots of work needs to get done around here, so I'm glad you're back. And no, I didn't think I had gotten rid of you, because I didn't. I only knocked you unconscious." "Oh, so you admit hitting me?" he asked with a raised eyebrow.

"Never said I didn't, did I?" she questioned back. "Well, good, 'cause I'm 'bout to write a report to everyone in Sector Command about you having a weapon at your desk," he said as he looked across and around her cubicle, searching.

Desiree had to laugh. She realized his pettiness and silliness. "I've saved you the stress, Steven. I have drafted a report myself to the Colony Head explaining how I accidentally knocked you unconscious over an intense argument we were having and agreed to bear the consequences of my office violation act. As such, I've served a query report form of my hours worked and rate of pay. My wages were deducted for the month. And no, I do not have any weapons at my desk. It's an arm exercise tool. Happy? Now let us get to work, thank you."

But Steven wasn't letting go that quickly. "You do have a weapon," he insisted. Pointing at the kettlebell, he exclaimed, "Look! What do you call this metal thing here?"

Desiree shook her head. What nonsense was this ant spewing? "It's a kettlebell. As I said, it's an exercise weight to keep my arms strong."

"I don't care whatcha call it. You struck me with it with intent to harm."

Gretchen sighed in exasperation. "Really, Steven," she moaned. "You honestly don't get it, do you?" She shook her head.

"Get what?" he asked curiously.

"You, Steven, you!"

"Me?! Me what?"

Gretchen sighed. She had enjoyed every single moment he was up in the hospital, and she saw the reason now. He was uncouth, loud, and mostly didn't even know what he was talking about. She decided to put him in his place. If he would not change and if no one told him what he was, she would do him the favor.

"No one likes you around here or anywhere else for that matter, Steven. You were 'handpicked' because the Ant General wanted you out of the way, to keep you away from his sight. Everyone considers you an obnoxious asshole, and the only reason no one says it is because they are too pissed to bother, but they say it behind you all the time. Everyone I know that has come across you finds you rude, annoying or a complaining bug. That is why no one wants to be around you."

Steven was visibly taken back by this revelation, and Desiree wondered why. It was clear, but somehow only Steven didn't see it. Why was he making her feel as though she had just said something he didn't know about? Wasn't that why he continued to be such a pest in everyone's lives?

"Look, when I wrote the report to report myself and what happened, I did it to avoid getting into trouble and hopefully get transferred. I was sick and tired of working with you, and I didn't want to be here when the doctor certified you okay to go home and back to work. Guess what, I got praised for standing up to you and teaching you a lesson. You weren't even supposed to be back to work here yet. My guess is the doc must have released you early or something."

Steven looked like he had just come to a sudden realization. "Yeah, he did," he revealed.

Desiree sighed again. "You see, Steven. The doctor was probably tired of you and your pesky nature." She wanted to continue, but the look on his face made her think she was a little too harsh on him. She decided to soft-pedal a little. He didn't know and needed help seeing it.

"See," she continued, "you're a great guy, and you have some decent skills, but your attitude sucks – a lot. You're not as funny as you think you are. You say inappropriate things in the wrong place and at the wrong time. You don't apologize when you should. You seek attention, always wanting everyone to know you are in the room.

"But people don't tell you anything because you seem to like doing all the talking. I am sorry I hit you with my kettlebell. I was angry. Everyone is so used to your poor attitude that they have come to accept it. I couldn't, so I reacted, and for that, Steven, I am sorry. Please work on yourself and let's try to get work done around here as well. We have a deadline to meet your needs and get your colony up and running."

Steven had never been so quiet and attentive this long before. He looked at Desiree and took in everything she said. He had absolutely no idea how she felt, or what any of them thought of him. He said quietly, "I never knew…"

She smiled; the soft smile a mother gives a child she has just scolded but was warming up to once more. "Now you know."

"Where do I start?" he asked, looking confused.

Still smiling she said, "Start at your cubicle, get some real work done and when we are done for the day,

Gretchen and I will walk you through some interesting lessons. Whatcha say?"

"Sounds like a plan," Steven said with a broad smile as he moved closer to hug Desiree standing with her wings and middle legs outstretched.

"Thank you," he said, shaking her foreleg when they separated from the hug. "And I am deeply sorry for being such a pest of a bug."

"That's the spirit, Steven!" Desiree said happily.

Steven entered his cubicle, feeling a warm glow spread through his heart.

ACKNOWLEDGMENTS

Everyday writing is hard enough. Writing about a story you have conjured up in your mind is even harder. I could not have completed this book without the help of so many others. Much credit to Editor, Michelle Rascon, for her keen eye, structure, and patience. Beta Reader, Luis Andrepres, for all the advice and suggestions on how words work. Proof Reader, Kit Duncan for such detailed feedback, professionalism, and awesome communication. Cover designer, Sam Johnson (illustrationalpal), for all her patience. Credit me with all the rest. Thank God for everything.

ABOUT THE AUTHOR

"Do one thing every day that scares you."
Eleanor Roosevelt

just Deirdre was born in New Orleans, Louisiana and grew up in Kansas City. She has moved around a bit until finally settling in Alabama. She has been with her significant other for twenty years. Deirdre has three adult children, four grandchildren, and one granddog who live in Georgia.

A graduate from FL Schlagle High, Deirdre was a single parent and worked hard to support her family. At the age of forty, she returned to school to further her education. Six years later she obtained a master's degree in Business Administration from Strayer University. By day, Deirdre is a government employee, but in her spare time, her creative writing alter ego, Petite Breaux, takes center stage.

Since then, and under that pseudonym, Deirdre has written a memoir *"Slightly Bruised and a Little Broken"*, a short story "The Whispering of My Heart" and a children's book *"Fun with Grandma"*. She is currently working on more short stories, adult novels and a suspense novel using her just Deirdre. name.

When she gets the time and has the inclination, Deirdre enjoys working out at her local gym. She enjoys watching TV, movies, and she also reads daily and takes time practicing meditating to rejuvenate her soul.

Deirdre enjoys going on vacation, with cruising being her favorite pastime. She lives life to the max and has done some of the things that scare her, like ziplining and parasailing. She plans to do a skydive one day.

OTHER BOOKS BY
THE AUTHOR just Deirdre.

2019 New Releases

A Variety of Short Stories/Novelettes (Drama /Humor)

Something Inside (Novel / Suspense / Family / Humor)

Other Coming Releases End of 2019, beginning 2020

Kallista, The Forbidden One
(Dark Fantasy/ Erotica/Vampire)

The Journal: The Nancy Bremen Story
(Suspense/Drama/ Family)

You can contact just Deirdre. or follow her at:

https://www.petitebreaux.com
petitebreaux@yahoo.com
Twitter - @AuthorPetiteb
Facebook - @petitebreaux

The author requests you as the reader to post a review on one of your favorite online retailers Amazon, Smashwords, B&N etc. The feedback and support are most appreciated. It helps Indie authors gain recognition. Thank you in advance.

www.ingramcontent.com/pod-product-compliance
Lightning Source LLC
Chambersburg PA
CBHW070943120726
47908CB00005BA/1504